Faith

Cecile Labar

ReadersMagnet, LLC

Faith
Copyright © 2024 by Cecile Labar

Published in the United States of America
ISBN Paperback: 978-1-954371-06-4
ISBN eBook: 978-1-954371-07-1

All rights reserved. No part of this publication may be reproduced, stored in a retrieval system or transmitted in any way by any means, electronic, mechanical, photocopy, recording or otherwise without the prior permission of the author except as provided by USA copyright law.

The opinions expressed by the author are not necessarily those of ReadersMagnet, LLC.

ReadersMagnet, LLC
10620 Treena Street, Suite 230 | San Diego, California, 92131 USA
1.619.354.2643 | www.readersmagnet.com

Book design copyright © 2024 by ReadersMagnet, LLC. All rights reserved.
Cover design by Ericka Obando
Interior design by Don De Guzman

About the Author

Cecile Angela Labar

I was born in Kingston, Jamaica in 1956. My family migrated to London England, when I nine years old. I studied at Croydon College for the certificate of qualification in Social Work, 1983-1985. I was divorced in 1985 after an eight-year marriage. I worked as an Education Welfare Officer/ Education Social Worker from 1986-1990. I studied at the Center of the Media Arts, Manhattan, New York in 1991-1991, and obtained a diploma in Broadcast Announcing division. I returned to London and soon became pregnant, I am the mother of a son, my first and only child.

I was a member of the Writers' Guild of Great Britain and New Producers alliance. I had a film company named Blossom Films, and had read a several books on how to write books and screenplays. My first book is titled Faith and my second book is titled Executive Producer; both these were never published. I finished the final draft of Faith in October 2020. My first screenplay was finished in 2000, and was titled Amazing Caring Girls, this was changed to Amazing Caring Woman; and has been adapted to a stage play in 2017. It is sold on Amazon and Barns & Noble. My second screenplay, titled Time Mission was finished in July 2020. I have written poems these were published, by Page Publishing, Poetry Anthology Volume 4; also sold on Amazon and Barns & Noble, and lyrics and treatments, these are for television.

I was baptized when my son was five months old, at Brown Hill Road Baptist Church. My church life began When living in Jamaica with my grandparents, my grandmother was a Christian and she took me to her Church and had taught me the 23rd psalms, this I remember by heart. At the age of 10 to 17 my brother Winston and Sister Annette went to Brown Hill Road Baptist Church, I cannot remember picking up the Bible to read from it. During the time of sermon, us youngster and teenagers would go to rooms at the back of the church, where we were taught Bible stories. I went to the church youth club on a Monday evening. I remember our Sunday school teacher telling us that he was a blood donor, and this and advertisement made me become a blood donor; this was a few years after my divorce. When I was married there was not a Bible in our marital home.

I went to Brixton College for two years 17 to 19, To study for the Preliminary Certificate in Residential Care. I worked on Saturdays, and traveling to Brixton from Catford, each working day, made me tired, so Sunday became my rest day and I did not go to church. At the end of collage, our class celebrate it in a Pub, and it was there I met my husband to be, on a social occasion. He was one of the Lecturer at the college. We dated for a year and we got engaged, at the age of 20 he asked me to live with him and I was married at the age of 21. It was when I was separated pending divorce papers, that I started to attend Brown Hill Road Baptist Church again. It was at this church that my son's father and I brought our son for dedication, and it was there I was baptized.

I returned to live in New York, Long Island, with my son in 2001, my son came over in August, and I came over in November. I became a Seventh-day Adventist in 2011. I worked as a Cashier, then as a Home Health Aide from 2005, until I became disable in 2018 with arthritis in both knees, I also suffer from schizophrenia, and high blood pressure.

About the Book

I began writing the book Faith in New Cross, London, England. I did the second draft in 2004 and completed it in October 2020. The book Faith gives my experiences in reading the Bible for the first time and my guidance by the Holy Spirit, also known as Counselor; since my baptism. Also realizing that a religious human being needs to grow into an educated, healthy person, and needs to grow in their faith; in doing so, I include the apostle Paul's teaching on faith. I tell of the dream I had before my baptism and the visions had after; one of them was seeing Lord Emmanuel.

I write about how the Bible had help me to make my baptism garments, using one hundred per cent white cotton fabric, making three different garments, with a good size hem, under wear, slip and top garment. I write about being baptized in the name of the Father, Son and Holy Spirit.

I write about Christians who read the gospel and not the Old Testament do not know God. I also write about the visions I had in seeing Satan, in my flat, whilst living in

New Cross, London, and the vision I had when seeing the devil, in New York.

I write about the things I found when reviewing three different Bibles. I wrote about what a church offers to its congregation, and write about how house group and counselling, can be beneficial to a religious person. I also mentioned Pastor Oral Roberts teaching on fear, and I had added Bible references.

Faith

As each individual human being needs to grow and develop into an educated, healthy human being, so does a religious human being need to grow in their faith. (Hebrews 11: 1-40). Our growth starts in our knowledge of the Bible, God Almighty's truth. The Bible gives us a true history of the creation of Heaven, Earth, and Humanity. It tells us the correct prophecy, of the ages to come, and it teaches us how to be saved and how to live a Godly life.

When we make a commitment to Lord God Almighty, we put away hate in our hearts, and learn to live in harmony with our family members, and brothers and sisters in the faith. Whatever sacrifices we must make, we make them for God Almighty and Lord Emmanuel's sake. It might mean putting God Almighty before our parents, friends, husband, wife, children, and brethren. In our society today, some cults and churches have used the scriptures, to get their own disciples to turn on their families, and give allegiance to cult groups. This was seen in the tragic massacre in Waco, Texas, USA. Such teachings are false and out of harmony with the scriptures.

In February 1993 the Waco siege began, when a government raid on a compound, led to a 51 days standoff between federal agents and members of a millennial Christian sect, called The Branch Davidians. They began to exchange heavy gunfire at the site. The siege ended dramatically on April 19th, 1993, when fires consumed the compound, leaving some 75 people dead, including 25 children.

David Koresh, the leader believed he could speak to God, and prophesized about the second coming of Christ. As well as the imminent end of the world. He converted more than 100 people and convinced them to live in the compound. David Koresh was considered a highly controversial figure, he used his position in the group to have sex with multiple wives, including girls as young as ten.

The first act of disobedience to God Almighty took place in the Garden of Eden by Adam and Eve. By their disobedience, many were made sinners, face with temptations, murders, sexually immoral, and sufferings. By obedience to God Almighty, many become righteous. We as righteous people grow in faith, through our help from God Almighty and Lord Emmanuel, if we are able to recognize the help given, and in doing so help the children of our branches, (John 15: 5, 15: 12). When I was baptized, I made my garments using one hundred percent white cotton fabric, with white cotton thread, with a good size hem; one was my underwear, the other was a full slip, using a thinner cotton fabric, and my top garment.

Water baptism means we are on the way to salvation. Lord Emmanuel was baptized by immersion, in the river Jordan. To be baptized is to be soaked in water, (John 3: 5, 8). And when we experience the spiritual birth, in the name of the Father, the Son and the Holy Spirit; then there is hope for a spiritual life, (Act 2: 38,39). Before and since my baptism I had received visions and help from a good Holy Spirit. (Act 2: 17). Before: Was a dream of pink baby rabbits in a straw bed; I did not understand the dream at the time. However, as a young teenager I had two pet rabbits, and they had babies. this was years Before I met Felix, the father of our son Ozias. We cannot hide nor deny our sins to God Almighty. Therefore, we repent of our sins through repentance and atonement. Our new life is no longer about living a life of sin. And we then strive not to be racist, sexist, nor discriminate against people with disabilities. We live out our lives serving God Almighty and Lord Emmanuel with clean thought and heart.

We as true believers must hold on to God Almighty's Peace, Love, Loyalty, and Faithfulness. As we learn to forsake all others in God Almighty's name, and in the strength of his son Lord Emmanuel, who overcome persecution, suffering, temptation, and death. Our reward is in the hope of a Heavenly reward, (Revelation 2: 10).

An important way of seeing God Almighty's prophecy is from Peter's Vision (Acts 10: 9-16). God Almighty knew that is people would move on to other countries, where animals such as reptiles would be in abundance. Therefore, God Almighty prepared the way, and made these clean to eat.

God Almighty's message here, (Acts 10: 38). Is that those that are circumcised and baptized, are sons and daughters of God Almighty, and Lord Emmanuel, Lord God anointed Lord Emmanuel with the Holy Spirit, and with this power he healed those that were oppressed by the devil.

The cross was made from a tree, the tree also means a family tree, Lord Emmanuel descendants came from Abraham to King David, (Matthew 1: 1-16), and he was clearly named Emmanuel by Lord God, before his birth. (Matthew 1: 22,23). We read in the Bible that Lord Emmanuel had mighty powers, yet he did not fight physically, nor used his mighty powers to save his own life, instead, when confronted with his forth coming death, by King Herod armed forces, Lord Emmanuel said he would lay down his life for us. (Matthew 15: 13). It was also Lord God will for Lord Emmanuel to return to the kingdom of Heaven. Lord Emmanuel died by the wicked evil powers and laws of King Herod. Pontius Pilate was a governor of King Herod armed forces.

The scriptures tell us that God Almighty, is Lord of Israel (Exodus 5:1), (Exodus 20: 2,3,4,6). Israel is a country where Lord God had promised his people when he brought them out of Egypt. Lord God had nurtured his people in his teachings long before Lord Emmanuel's birth. Lord God had sent his servants to choose good people from his countries, but those servants were either wounded or killed. Lord God also sent his son Lord Emmanuel, whom they killed, (Mark 12: 1,12). We, as true believers, sing glory and praise when, Lord Emmanuel was resurrected from death. Lord Emmanuel is our Lord (John 20: 18).

Many people pray for Lord Emmanuel to return to Earth. Yet, some people did not accept Lord Emmanuel during his time on Earth. People questioned whether he was the son of Lord God and whether he was the Messiah, although Lord Emmanuel had done many miracles. What will people do today, when so many of Lord God's commandments and laws are broken; by wicked, evil, corrupt people? We must remember that Lord Emmanuel was betrayed, (John 18: 1, 5). And was killed by mortal human beings, and should we consider Judas's death, to be the will of God, (Acts 1: 16, 18).and we hold in our heart hateful feelings for Lord God, then we must remember that God Almighty is a Good God, and a God of justice.

In the Revised Standard Version Bible, (Matthew 11: 11,12) tell us that violent men as taken over the Kingdom of Heaven by force. Yet this hardly seems true, when we read of God Almighty's powers, and know of the moral behavior he expects from us, and the commandments and laws he expects us to obey and the tithe offering and prayers that are pleasing to him. Would he then not cast out violent men from Heaven? Lord Emmanuel left us a prayer, known as the Lord's prayer, this Bible says. "forgive us our debit as we forgive our debtors," when it is clearly "forgive our trespasses as we forgive our trespasser." (Matthew 6: 9,12). If we say we have not sinned, we make him out to be a liar. (1 John 1: 10). Some Christians say forgive our sins in thought, words, and deeds.

When Lord Emmanuel was born, he was circumcised on the eighth day of his birth, and an offering of a goat and a lamb were made, not two turtledoves or two pigeons, (Luke 2: 21,24). When the three wise men visited, they had presented gifts of gold, frankincense, and myrrh, (Matthew 2:11). The shepherds would have brought a lamb out of lovingkindness. Sacrifices were to be offered, along with an attitude of 'trust' and thankfulness. The offering was taken to the tabernacle, and the Holy man made the sacrifice; and the sin would not happen again. A turtledove or a pigeon would have been accepted for poor people who could not afford to sacrifice a large animal. (Leviticus 5:7).

When Lord Emmanuel was with us on Earth, his teaching was of 'Love' for our fellow men and women (1 John 4: 7,10). God Almighty had promised us a New Heaven and a New Earth, (Isaiah 65:17). Obtaining a New Heaven and a New Earth, would surely help us believers to feel safe in a peaceful world; (Revelations 10: 1,7).

People born out of wedlock cannot enter the Holy Land, Israel, similarly, "woman who are married, and have children by another man; the woman has disobeyed the law of God Almighty. She committed adultery, and her children will strike no root, and her branches will bear no fruit. "New Jerusalem Bible, (Ecclesiasticus 23: 22-37). The first child belongs to God, the first calf, the first elephant, whale, seal, land, people, and book, in fact the first of everything belong to God.

Historically, we are aware of how many countries, including African countries, where their land was taken at the hands of wicked, evil, covetous people. These people were tortured, sold into slavery and shipped to other countries. Many of these people were killed by hanging. When Lord God people came out of Egypt, many of these people were Negroid. The Israelites had Negroid servants, and they were also of the faith, according to Lord God's covenant and Laws. God Almighty said he would not give false prophecy, (Ezekiel 12: 21,28). In one of my visions, I saw a black man, so I know there are black people in Heaven.

The sacred scriptures were translated from Hebrew into Aramaic, Greek, Latin, English and many other languages. With these translations we gained some rather obscure meaning of the original words. I have reviewed three different translations of the sacred scriptures, our precious gift, the Bible. The New International Version, by Hodder and Stoughton, published in 1983. The Good News Bible, by the bible Societies, published by Collins in 1976, and the Revised Standard Version, published by Collins in 1901. God tell us in the Bible, that nothing should be added to it, and nothing should be taken from it. I have found the New International Version to be readable, with introductory help. It does not have all the books of the Bible, but it has the Hebrew alphabets in some of the Psalms. However, some words are not appropriate, for instance, (Mark 9: 7) says "A cloud appeared and enveloped them" rather than, "a cloud overshadowed them," as in the Revised Standard Version Bible. Members of a church are given envelopes to put their tithes in.

The Good News Bible is also readable, with introductory help and illustrations, written in what is known as today's

English. It loses some of the correct history of the Bible. (Deuteronomy 27: 11-26), refers to "God's curse" rather than "cursed be he who dishonors his father or his mother." And all the people shall say 'Amen' as in the Revised Standard Version Bible. In fact, Lord Emmanuel had cursed, (Mark 11:14, Mark 11: 20-22). Therefore, pray to Lord God and Lord Emmanuel for any curses to be remove from us. We, as Christian, do not curse, we rebuke them.

Finally, once again, the Revised Standard Version, is readable, and has alternative meaning of words from the Hebrew and Greek translations. Although some words are not appropriate when thinking of the history of the Bible. For example, (Mark 9: 5). The word "booths." The word tent or sukkah would have been more appropriate. After all, we use the word Halleluiah and this is a Hebrew word. (Leviticus 23: 40-43). We were to dwell in sukkah, as a shelter made from branches of palm trees.

Today, we have many different churches, with different ways of worshipping. Seventh Day Adventist, Church of Christ, Catholic Church, Church of England, Pentecostal Church, Baptist Church, Jehovah Witness Church, Synagogue, and Mosque. Whilst all these churches, Synagogues, and Mosques believe in the same God, the Jews and Muslins only pray to God. The Jews and Muslins has an historical way of worshiping. Lord Emmanuel said, "love God," and he did not come to abolish the laws and the Prophets but to complete them.

The Church of Christ believe in full immersion baptism, but they drink water instead of wine for the Lord's Supper, also known as communion. (John 4: 13,14). This kind of worshipping is not in harmony with the Lord's teaching. Some churches drink grape juice instead of wine for communion and tell their congregation that it is grape juice, Lord Emmanuel drank for the Lord's Supper. not wine, when we read the Bible, we know He drank wine. (John 2: 1-11). After all, it is only a small miniature glass of wine.

The Jews refer to God as Lord and King, El Shaddai, a Hebrew name for God Almighty, (Genesis 48: 3). The Revised Standard Version Bible. Some Christians says Lord God Almighty, (Revelation 4:8). The letters, YHWH is found in Exodus 4, foot notes, Exodus 3:14, are the words "I am," the letters YHWH when spelled with capital letters, stand for the divine name. The Hebrew meaning is not by a mighty hand, the verb is Hayah. YHWH in Hebrew also means Yahweh, and this means Lord. The Jehovah Witness had changed the letters, YHWH into the word Jehovah; why make up another name when Hayah or Yahweh is pronounceable? Church of England and Catholic churches refer to God as Almighty God, an expression not found in the sacred scriptures. Lord Emmanuel is referred to as the Messiah, Rabbi, and Jesus Christ; the name Jesus means "Savior," and the name Christ means "Anointed one," the name Emmanuel means "God is with us."

I have read the Holy Quran, and I found no reference to terrorism being acceptable. When the Muslins greet each other, they say Shalom alai kun, in Nigerian, meaning peace be upon you; and the name Allah mean God in Arabic. The Catholics end their prayer by saying, in the name of the Father, Son, and Holy Spirit. The Catholics also pray to the Virgin Mary. Why pray to Mary, when she was only a bless woman? They also encourage their congregation to pray to other Saints. Not even the apostle Paul asked us to pray to him. As for Priest, the Laws handed down to Moses says Priest shall not marry a woman divorced from her husband or woman who are harlot or defiled. Catholics, Christians, Jews, and Muslims say Amen, this means "so be it," "Certainty," "Truth" and "Verily," (Jeremiah 11: 3-5). The word Amen is found in Psalms 41 and 106. Was this word written with reference to a sin mentioned in (Deuteronomy 27: 15-26)? The apostle Paul had used this word, (Romans 11:36), could this be why so many churches use this word, after a prayer, a sermon, a Hymn, and after reading the Bible? I believe this word is inoperative, if used at random; a word far better remaining in its dynamic functioning system. Since God Almighty said, he is the Alpha and the Omega, (Revelation 21:5-8). Lord God is at the beginning of our prayers, so should be Lord Emmanuel, Lord God, and Lord Emmanuel are the judge of our prayers. Surely words like Halleluiah, Selah, and Shalom should be at the end of our prayers. Halleluiah means Praise the Lord, Selah means Forever, and shalom means peace. Lord God and Lord Emmanuel are the judge of our prayers, (Psalms 9: 3,4). In many countries, modern society have failed to worship on the Holy Day, the Sabbath Day, this is on a Saturday, it begins on a Friday evening, at sunset, and it ends on a Saturday evening, at sunset, (Genesis 1: 5). Also, the new year, given to us by Lord God, that is in April, (Exodus 12: 1-3).

The Roman Emperor Constantine declared Christianity as the official religion of the Empire. He issued numerous laws relating to Christian practices and susceptibilities; for instance, abolishing the penalty of crucifixion and the practice of branding certain criminals; also enjoying the observance of Sunday worshiping and Saints-day; and extending privileges to the clergy while suppressing at least some offensive pagan practices. The early church had worshiped on the Sabbath.

The Bible informs us about unacceptable behavior, this is found in (Genesis 19:30-38) and in (Revelation 22: 18,19). The soul is something that is untouchable, not to be misinterpreted by men, who have a weakness of loving each other sexually; here was an admiration for David by Jonathan because he had won a battle from the enemy. They both knew that God Almighty, had denounced such behavior. (1 Samuel 18: 1-4). God Almighty had denounced killing, yet in our modern society, we see much killing; not only from young people, but adults and people who enforcing the law. (2 Samuel 2: 23-26). It is an abomination for men or woman to indulge themselves in homosexuality, lesbianism or unnatural copulation between man and woman is an abomination. Any form of sorcery is an abomination. We should not make any markings on the face or body, this includes tattoo.

Upland pregnancy can be solved by Lord God or Lord Emmanuel, I experienced this. I was pregnant although I had vomited, and saw the vision of a baby's face that looked like me. It was when I realized that I had not seen my period for two months; that it came to light. Lord Emmanuel took it away. I was living at Arbuthnot Road, New Cross, London, and Felix was the father. I believe it was taken away because I was baptized and I was not married to him, and maybe Lord God would only accept one child born out of wedlock. In fact, the book of Samuel tells us of many sins, from conspiracy, (2 Samuel 13: 3-5, 12-14), theft, (2 Samuel 15:6), betrayal, (2 Samuel 16: 20-23), lies, (1 Kings 3: 16-28) and unlawful circumcises, (1 Samuel 18: 25).

The Bible also tells us about acceptable behavior, such as dressing modestly, women dressing like women and men dressing like men. Since Abraham God Almighty had kept his covenant with the Hebrew, Israelite, Samaritan, and Jewish people; and with those who abide by Lord Emmanuel's teaching. The Hebrew, Israelite, and blood descendants, are now living all over the world (Genesis 17: 9-13).

The garden of Eden was in Iraq, and Mesopotamia is now Iraq and was the cradle of civilization. Noah built the Art in Iraq, and the tower of Babel was in Iraq. Abraham was from Ur, this is in southern Iraq. Iraq means "country with deep roots." Isaac's wife Rebekah is from Nahor this is in Iraq. Jacob met Rachel in Iraq, and Jonah preached in Nineveh, which is in Iraq. Assyria, which is in Iraq, conquered the ten tribes of Israel. Amos cried out in Iraq, Babylon, which is in Iraq destroy Jerusalem. Daniel was in the lion's den in Iraq. The three Hebrew children were in the fire in Iraq. Belshazzar, the King of Babylon, saw the 'writings on the wall' in Iraq, and Nebuchadnezzar, King of Babylon carried the Jews captive into Iraq. Ezekiel preached in Iraq. The wise men were from Iraq. Peter preached in Iraq, and the 'Empire' of man,' described in Revelation is called Babylon, this was a city in Iraq, Iraq is not the name used in the Bible, the Bible name are Babylon, Chaldean, Land of Shinar, and Mesopotamia. The word Mesopotamia means between the two rivers, more exactly between the Tigris and Euphrates rivers.

God's people are known as the twelve tribes. Historian have speculated about how people had migrated; some believe the pyramids in south America, were built by the Aztec civilization. It could have been built by people who had traveled there from Egypt. Geologist have maintained that the continent where closer together, and that is why the Aborigines became an isolated tribe. There are some Jews who do not attend to the wounded, or go to graveyards; they are known as Cohen. Such people should have compassion, when it come to the wounded. (Luke 10: 30-37).

Some Christians think there is only these books in the Bible for them: The Gospel. These Christians who only read the Gospel, in my opinion will never know God Almighty. Lord Emmanuel said "to know me is to know my father," meaning he look like his father, (John 14: 7), and he had read the Old Testaments.

In some parts of the world today, we face with corruption and violation of people's rights. These sorts of people do not know God Almighty; if they did, they would change their behavior. Soul had persecuted the early Christian, and he began to see what sin had done to him, (Acts 1:16. Acts 26: 12-20). We have seen a repeat of such persecutions when the Germans persecuted the Jews. People today can become so completely occupied, with living in the world of sin, they cannot see nor understand the way God Almighty wants them to live, (Exodus 20: 1-17). Today, we have Judges and laws to deal with people who breaks the rules. Many are put into prisons. Should these Judges fail in their duties, then God Almighty, who gave us commandments and laws, has his own way of dealing with evil, wicked, corrupt people. (Genesis 6: 11-22, Genesis 7: 1-5). Also, if some of us knew what Satan or the devil look like, we would understand God Almighty punishment. Whilst living in New Cross, London, in a vision I saw Satan, in my living room, Satan had two horns on the top of his head, about five inches long; he was also handsome. I saw the devil in a vision in New York whilst dating a man who turned out to have the devil within him. This was in 2003. The devil shows me his thumb; it was dark, bumpy skin, with pointed finger nail. They are two different creatures.

Lord Emmanuel, the Messiah, left us a prayer, known as the Lord's prayer. It tells us that the Earth is God's kingdom. Isaias 5. As worshippers must do the will of God on Earth. (Matthew 6: 9-13). Angels are servants of God Almighty and Lord Emmanuel, and they have done God's will in Heaven and on Earth. (Zechariah 4: 6, Matthew 13: 41-43), Lord Emmanuel also did God's will (John 5:30).

Having worshipped at several different churches and had lived in an area where there were seven churches within a two-mile radius, of New Cross, London. And some of these churches never had a full congregation. These were Saint Mary, Saint Anthony, a Catholic church, a Pentecostal church, Jehovah's Witness, a church held in a day center, and a Seventh day Adventist church. It could be said that some churches have a caring attitude toward their congregation. Some will travel to different areas, and to other countries to welcome new worshippers. The churches, mosques and synagogues are places where worshippers meet to pray, find strength in faith, further their knowledge of the scriptures, befriend each other, share their problems and anxieties, and offer to pray for each other. (James 4: 8-12). The religious message here is that God dwells by his spirit, within the hearts of every true believer. Therefore, prayer is a spiritual message, giving us spiritual strength. We then rely upon God's light, guidance, love, and peace, that dwells in our thoughts hearts.

Not everyone today has the spirit of Lord God. Not everyone hears his voice, have his dreams, have his visions, see his face, and know that they are loved by him. I am sure when God Almighty is ready, he will rest his spirit in those that are blessed, blameless and good. And in those who wholeheartedly want to change their lives and serve God; through his son, Lord Emmanuel. Therefore, we should believe in the power of prayer, (James 1: 5-8). Have we changed as a society? I think, yes, when we look back, at how the men of Lord God and Lord Emmanuel died: However, there are certain countries where it is dangerous to be a Christian

Matthew

Suffered martyrdom in Ethiopia and was killed by a sword wound.

Mark

Died in Alexandria, Egypt, after being dragged by horses through the streets until he was dead.

Luke

Was hanged in Greece because of his tremendous preaching to the lost.

John

Faced martyrdom when he was boiled in a huge basin of boiling oil during a wave of persecution in Rome. However, he was miraculously delivered from death. John was then sentenced to the mines on the prison Island of Patmos. He wrote his prophetic book of Revelation on Patmos. The apostle John was later freed and returned to serve as Bishop of Edessa in modern Turkey. He died as an old man, the only apostle to die peacefully.

FAITH

Peter

He was crucified upside down on an X-shape cross. According to church tradition, it was because he told his tormentors that he felt unworthy to die in the same way that Lord Emmanuel had died.

James

The leader of the church in Jerusalem was thrown over a hundred feet down, the southeast pinnacle of the temple when he refused to deny his faith in Emmanuel. When they discovered that he survived the fall, his enemies beat James to death with a fuller's club.

James the son of Zededee

As a strong leader of the church, James was beheaded at Jerusalem. The Roman Officer who guarded James, watched, amazed, as James defended his faith at his trial. Later the Officer walked beside James to the place of execution; overcome by conviction, he declared his new faith to the judge and knelt beside James to accept beheading as a Christian.

Bartholomew

Also known as Nathaniel was a missionary to Asia. He witnessed for our Lord in present-day Turkey.

Bartholomew was martyred for his preaching in Armenia, where he was flayed to death by a whip.

Andrew

Was crucified on an X-shape cross in Patras, Greece. After being whipped severely by seven soldiers, they tied his body to the cross with cords to prolong his agony. His followers reported that when he was led toward the cross, Andrew saluted it, saying. "I have long desired to expected this happy hour. The cross has been consecrated by the body of Emmanuel hanging on it." He continued to preach to his tormentors for two days until he expired.

Thomas

Was stabbed with a spear in India during one of his missionary trips to establish the church in the sub-continent.

Jude

Was killed with arrows when he refused to deny his faith in Emmanuel.

Matthias

The apostle chosen to replace the traitor Judas Iscariot, was stoned, and then beheaded.

Paul

Was tortured and then beheaded by the evil Emperor Nero at Rome in AD 67. Paul endured a lengthy imprisonment, which allowed him to write his many epistles to the churches he had formed throughout the Roman Empire. These letters, which taught many of the foundational doctrines of Christianity, form a large portion of the New Testament.

Perhaps this is a reminder to us that our suffering here is indeed minor compared to the intense persecution and cold cruelty faced by the apostles during their time, for the sake of the faith. And he shall be hated of all men for my name's sake; but he that perseveres all things, to the end shall be saved.

Brownhill Road Baptist Church

Catford, London.

This church has provided for the needs of every member, from the cradle to the grave; resources such as a crèche, and youth clubs. A loop system for the benefit of the hard of hearing, audio tapes of the sermon, information booklets of the week's events, prayer meetings and Bible study; held at the church, home Bible study fellowship, service for elderly friends, fellowship lunch, women's Bible study group, person to person visits, musical evenings, children's services, sympathy messages and prayer for the deceased.

Regular worshippers are given the opportunity, to become involved in the running and organizing of the church. Thus, having the feeling of belonging, as an extension of their family.

Events such as leaderships, coffee rote, church cleaning, flower arrangements, tear fund and other charitable organizations

House Groups

Saint Mary's church,
New Cross, London.

The aims of these groups are to create an opportunity, for individual members to meet and grow spiritually, in sharing their knowledge of the Bible. Prayers are often said at these group. Also, Bible studies are held, tea, coffee, and cookies are served. It is also a venue where a person can increase their faith against life's trouble. Here, Christians have been known to date each other and get married. A true believer can say bloody, they can hate a thing, weapon, person, or an action. We can also learn to forgive. (Ecclesiastes 3: 1-17)

In a group, every member is a potential helper, characterized by a common concern for individual members and their emotions. Help is achieved by the strengthening of an individual's state of mind, their self-concept, and their relationship with others. The need for reassurance and the confirmation of values, attitudes, and the support for the image we have of our selves is important. However, what we cloth ourselves in, is not the determining factor in some people's lives; that is poor people dress in what they can afford. and some religious groups, such as Jews and Muslims, they have rules, for how men and women should dress. It is criminal for people to associate the colors that innocent people ware, to manipulate situations for political power, or for what is in fashion.

It hardly seems acceptable, that in our world today, science and technology have taken men and women into space when, in some countries, poor people are still without housing, food, and items for personal hygiene. Therefore, affluent people should remember that Lord Emmanuel had helped the poor. (Matthew 14: 17-21). We as faithful followers, must also strive to help the poor. And strive to be perfect from Lord God's teaching, in the Holy Scriptures, and remember that no one is perfect.

There are other misinterpretations in the Bible that only powerful people could have will there. The Bible became assessable to all in 1539; before, only the Royal families and the Roman Catholic Church had knowledge of scriptures. Moses who gave us the food law, (Leviticus 11: 1-47). Lord Emmanuel knew these laws. Therefore, is message here was not about declaring all food clean. (Mark 7: 19), in the Revised Standard Version Bible. Other than what is mentioned in (Act 10: 6-9).

It hardly believable that Lord Emmanuel, knowing the law on divorce, and the ten commandments would have said; "I say unto you, that whosoever shall put away his wife, saving for the cause of fornication, causeth her to commit adultery; and whosoever shall marry her that is divorced committeth adultery." (Matthew 5: 31,32),

King James Version). I am sure Lord Emmanuel would have said, whoever, divorce and marries another, then love one another. There are some Christians who believe speaking in tongues is speaking gibberish. Speaking in tongues means speaking in a foreign language. (Acts 2: 4)

Counselling

Lord Emmanuel said he would send us a counselor (John 16: 7, 14: 26). When reading the Bible, I would read things then it would disappear. I have done some study in counselling, and for those who do not receive the Holy Spirit they may find is beneficial to see a Pastor.

Even the most 'normal' youngster/adult might seem utterly incomprehensible and inconsistent from time to time, and these aberrations can look like serious disturbance. their rapid mood changes, unpredictable out bursts, risky behavior, and resorts to fanatical activity, are the outward signs of their attempts to manage the resurgence of primitive anxieties and the stresses of loss and change. When they feel swamped, betrayed, scared, bereaved, defeated and shy. Even the fundamentally strong people, will appear to be extremely fragile and distressed at some point.

The delicate balance between being within and without the client dynamic system; of being Neither too close nor too remote is nicely conveyed. Kahn's statement in 1974. You have to suffer along with the client but not suffer like the client. Although it is important to stick closely to the interactions and to attend to the minute nuances of details, it is also important for the Counselor to stand well back in order to encompass the whole of the client's problem. It requires the apparently contradictory action, of letting go of yourself and remember who you are. It is crucial for the client, that the Counselor does not lose his/her personal boundaries, and get lost in his/her life, and be in touch within his/her self.

Keeping person boundaries intact, and maintain a helpful distance automatically ensure that the autonomy and individuality of the client are respected. The Counselor can allow the client to explore and discover their own life and experiences. And their own feelings, rather like certain parents can permit a child to explore without crowding their space; with warnings and encouragements, based on their own good/bad experiences and anxieties. Although there are some 'universalities' about people, each has his/her own idiosyncratic experience of those commonalities. The counselor might have some general assumptions, but he/she cannot presume about specific details; this can be discovered in the emotional response, in the interaction between the two as the session proceeds. Each client will react differently to a similar situation. Misunderstanding a client subjective experience, is forgivable but failing to try to see their uniqueness by applying assumptions is not forgivable; the client does not turn into a case textbook to be studied. The lack of human respect invites withdrawal of trust.

FAITH

The Catholic church has long provided spiritual counseling in their confession box. An individual confesses their sins, and prayers are said. However, the abuse, of children and people, such as child sexual abuse, mental abuse, physical abuse, sexually immoral, sorcerers, compulsive stealing, compulsive liars, drug trafficking or sex trafficking are often not resolved, because they believe Lord Emmanuel died for their sins. (John 8:34, John 3: 17, Mark 9: 42). Lord Emmanuel's wounds was foretold. (Isaiah 53).

Lord Emmanuel was a servant and son of Lord God, we should no doubt believe, that the Holy Spirit of Lord God, are in Priests, Imams, Rabbis, Reverends, Vicars, Pastors, and Worshippers, who truly believes (Numbers 11: 16,17). The Holy Spirit is not always in Reverends and Worshippers that are married. Therefore, married couples should not deny themselves to each other, unless they agree to do so for a while in order to spend their time in prayer, and fasting, and during the time when a wife is on her menstruation. (John 15: 5).

God Almighty is the master of fear and the fearful. Human being has a tendency to fear; when the unknown, crosses our path we become afraid. Yet we should fear God because we know what He can do. Lord God not only conquered fear, He also conquered the fearful. (Daniel 6: 22). Lord God mastered the people who were bound by fear. True believers do not worry about using two letters, such as two 'L,' or two 'M' in a word, or name, because two men's name is mentioned in our prayers, and we love them: Lord God and Lord Emmanuel. If they consider two 'M' to be associated with two mothers then, remember Naamah, wife of Noah was a blessed mother, so was the Virgin Mary, a blessed mother.

An individual with an anxiety problem, a fear, and stress related problem, mighty find it more beneficial to talk to a member of the clergy, rather than a family member, friend, social worker or colleague. Especially if they are looking for spiritual help and guidance with problem like the following:

Inspiration from the words Pastor Oral Roberts.

Fear of Failure: Most good things that are never done are left undone because of someone's fear. The worse failure is not being willing to try what you believe God wants you to do.

Fear of Poverty: We often become grasping and greedy in our efforts to stay ahead of poverty, yet we can acquire material goods and money by using our faith. when I moved into my flat, in New Cross, London, the only furnisher I had was a bed and a crib for my son; the living room was empty. I attended Saint Mary's church, and the Vicar visited me, we talk standing up in the living room. When he visited me again, he brought me a chair so I would have something to set on. The other thing I did before my flat was painted, was to go to the Catholic church and ask the Priest to cleans and bless my flat. He prayed and sprinkled Holy water in every room. I gave him my son's dedication gown for the poor.

My flat was wall papered and painted by my older brother, Anthony, and Felix, whose real name is Fidelis, my son's father. My younger brother Winston, paid my older brother to do the work on my flat; he also gave me a play pen for my son. I acquired carpets for the rooms and a second-hand table and chairs from my mother, Lottie Labarr, who gave me money; a couch and arm chairs from my younger sister, Annette; and furniture for my son's room from my sister Paulette, who lives in America. I brought fabric for curtains and made curtains for the rooms. I was given and allowance by the government for moving, and this brought my stereo record player; I already had a television. I also brought other things, such as a ladder, a high chair for my son and a safety gate for the stairs. Also a few things for the kitchen. And, of course, the paint and wall paper.

It was at this flat, that I read the Bible for the first time, from Genesis to Revelation, and I was guided by the Holy Spirit. I prayed to know the truth. After four years of living in my flat. I had a vision of Lord Emmanuel. He was standing and was dressed in a long uncooked oat meal-color garment; with long white hair, (white people's hair), I did not see his face because white cloud covered it. All these things happen to me by having faith, and I say praise the Lord, and offer prayers of thankfulness.

Fear of Criticism: This fear is one of the worst fears we allow ourselves to develop. what people say about us is important because it is reflected in the way we are treated by others. It is wrong, however, to make their opinion of us the determining factor in our lives; if it is impossible to change a situation at that time. Lord Emmanuel said, "father forgive them, for they know not what they do." When nailed on the wooden cross. (Luke 23:34, Matthew 11:19).

Fear of Betrayal: The fear of being hurt or betrayed by someone special can be overcome by faith. Just because a human being is hurt by someone special to them, there is no reason for a human being to stop believing in people and find someone new.

Fear of Sickness: It is a known fact, that those who worry and fret over their health, are sick sooner or later. It is a greater miracle to stay well and not need healing (Exodus 15:26).

Fear of Not Being Appreciated: This can cause us a lot of misery, but in most cases, it is caused by our wrong believing. Few people will go out of their way to tell you, their appreciation. A human being must remember their little gifts of kindness, and to be appreciated one must appreciate others. We believers, appreciate Lord God and Lord Emmanuel. (Psalms 92). In the Jewish prayer book, there is no horn or mythological creature in the Sabbath day prayer. (King James Version).

Fear of Old Age: This alarms people. Not being able to accept changes with aging that causes the problem. It is possible to help old people to grow into old age, with sustaining mercy, patience, and growing faith. (Ecclesiastes 7:1). True faith, Lord God and Lord Emmanuel, will conquer all these fears and set a human being free. (Hebrew 11: 1-12). Lord Emmanuel is also interested in our health; he had healed many people. (Mark 5: 34, 42; John 9: 1,13).

Some parents are so fearful they often fail to help their children to socialize with others because of their own inadequacy. Through counseling a human being can try to locate the specific troublesome problem and help an individual to change their behavior, attitude, and values. Allowing the individual to discuss them unique past and drawing out painful memories, allows the client to see the stumbling block, or reason for aggressive or deviant behavior. Good regards and trust is essential in counseling.

Everyone inherits both the good and bad qualities from their parents through their DNA in their genes. However, this does not mean that parents who displayed behavioral problems in their youth does not mean their children will grow up and display the same behavioral problems. People not only suffer for their own sins, they sometimes suffer because of the sins of their father or mother this does not happen once you give your heart to the Lord. Therefore, by faith we obey Lord God and Lord Emmanuel's teaching. Lord God disciplines those he loves, (Hebrews 12:5,6). This suffering was only for four generations; it is not a suffering planned or manipulated by mortal human beings. It does not count if the sons or daughters have piousness.

This is a prayer I had written when my son was in high school. He is now married with a daughter of one year and four months, and they are expecting a baby son.

God Almighty, our Lord, blessed be your Holy name Yahweh. You are the great I am. It is our duty to praise you, and glorify you, and thank you. You are our everlasting rock.

I pray in the name of Lord Emmanuel, our Holy one, blessed be he. He is known as Jesus Christ. Lord Emmanuel by your words, you have brought me out of darkness into your Holy light. Please do not make me go astray. I thank God for giving us the Holy Bible and established in us eternal life.

I pray for Lord God's people. The house of Israel. Lord God being merciful, forgiving iniquities, and does not destroy repeatedly. For you O' God, and Lord Emmanuel are good and forgiving, and abounding in lovingkindness to all who call on you.

I pray my name is written in the book of life. My God so love fallen men that he gave his only begotten son, Lord Emmanuel, not only to live among men, but to bear their sins. As it is written in (John 1:29). "Behold the lamb of God, who takes away the sins of the world."

May Lord God who blessed our fathers, Abraham, Isaac, and Jacob, bless the congregation of New Jerusalem Seventh-day Adventist church, bless their husbands, wives, sons, and daughters, and all that belongs to them. May Lord God remember all the churches I had attended and worship at, before finding a Seventh-day Adventist church. Also, those who provide food and charity for the poor and all who faithfully occupy themselves with the need of the community. May the Holy one, blessed be he, give them their reward, may he remove from them all sickness, heal their body, and forgive their sins. May Lord God send blessing and success in all their activities along with all Israel.

FAITH

Lord Emmanuel, you said to your disciples, "What things so ever you desire, when you pray believe that you receive them and you shall have them." (Mark 11: 24) Lord Emmanuel, you said, "You shall ask in my name and I say onto you, that I will pray to the father for you, for the father himself loveth you, I have chosen you, that what-ever you shall ask of the father in my name. He may giveth you." (John 16:26,27, John 15:16). It is written, "No one can come to me unless the Father who sent me draws him; and I will raise him up at the last day." (John 6: 44). Lord Emmanuel you also said, "Ask and it will be given to you, "knock and it will be opened to you," and "seek and you will find." (Matthew 7:7).

Lord Emmanuel it is written that "It is easier for a camel to go through the eye of a needle, than for a rich man to enter the kingdom of God." (Mark 10: 25). Lord Emmanuel receiving four million, will help me to buy a house, a car for my son, and send my son to Law school, have some vacations, pay my bills, and keep me until I die. I would give money to charities, I would give money to my church, I would give money to my family members, I would give money to my son's father, and I would give money to my good friends. Lord Emmanuel, you said, "For all things are possible with God." (Mark 10:27). And, as it is written in (Ecclesiastes 10: 19), bread is made for laughter, and wine gladdens life, and money answers everything. (Revised Standard Version Bible).

Shalom.

www.ingramcontent.com/pod-product-compliance
Lightning Source LLC
LaVergne TN
LVHW020445080526
838202LV00055B/5336